Henry V

Captain Fluellen
Welsh captain

Duke of Exeter
Henry's uncle

Archbishop of Canterbury

John
Soldier

Cambridge, Scroop and Grey
Conspirators against Henry

Henry V
King of England

Earl of Westmorland
Supporter of Henry

Alexander
Soldier

Michael
Soldier

Princess Katherine
Charles VI's daughter

Katherine's maid

The Dauphin
Charles VI's son

Charles VI
King of France

Duke of Burgundy
French lord

Mistress Quickly
Pistol's wife

Pistol and Bardolph
Former friends of Henry

Serving boy

Timothy Knapman
Illustrated by Yaniv Shimony

King of England, King of France

Act one

Prince Hal had often been a worry to his father – and to the rest of England. While King Henry IV was busy ruling the country, his son spent his days with drunkards, liars and thieves. That wasn't how the heir to the throne should behave!

The worst of Prince Hal's friends was the fat and greedy knight Sir John Falstaff. Many people feared that when Hal became king he would fill his palaces with scoundrels and shower Falstaff with gold.

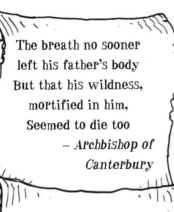

But when, at last, the old king died, something close to a miracle happened. Prince Hal turned his back on his old friends and their wicked ways. The moment the crown was placed on his head, he became everything a king should be.

He was suddenly wise, religious and brave – but how? Some people said the new king had just pretended to be wicked so that he could mix with the lowest of the low and find out what life was really like for his subjects. It was not something he would have learned if he'd stayed at court with his father. Being a bad prince had made him a better king.

Henry V was going to need all his wisdom and cunning as he set out on the great adventure of his reign. He believed that he was the rightful King of France as well as England. It was no surprise that the current King of France did not agree. If Henry wanted to take the French throne, he would have to fight for it.

Sitting with his great council, Henry asked the advice of the Archbishop of Canterbury.

"Be careful how you answer," he said. "If you tell me I have the right to be King of France, it will mean war – and many innocent people will die.

Therefore take heed...
How you awake
our sleeping sword
of war
– Henry V

I want to be certain our cause is just."

"Have no fear, sire," said the Archbishop. "You are the rightful King of France. Your ancestors won great glory fighting in this noble cause. Now it is time for you to do the same."

Henry's uncle, the Duke of Exeter, and his father's friend, the Earl of Westmorland, roared their approval. But Henry remained cautious.

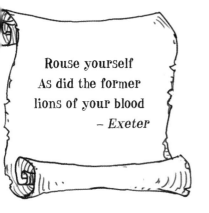

Rouse yourself
As did the former
lions of your blood
    – *Exeter*

"You know what happens whenever we send our army to France," he said. "The Scots take advantage and invade England."

"The French are weak, sire," said the Archbishop.

"You need only take a quarter of your troops with you and you will still conquer them easily. We can defend England with the rest."

Henry thought for a minute then he nodded his head. "Very well," he said. He summoned one of the soldiers standing guard by the door. "The French ambassador wanted to see us. Send him in."

The ambassador – usually a confident, charming man – was  trembling with fear. "Your M-Majesty," he stammered, "I bring word from the Dauphin, the son of the King of France. Before I speak, please understand that the message is his, not mine."

"Don't be afraid," said Henry. "I will not punish you for your master's words."

"Very well," said the ambassador. "The Dauphin says that you are young and foolish, and think this is all a game, but you should beware. You cannot just walk into France and take what you want. Instead, he sends you this treasure, which he thinks is more suitable for someone your age." The ambassador stretched out a shaking hand and pointed to a large chest.

"What's inside it, uncle?" Henry asked Exeter. Exeter opened the chest.

For a moment, he looked puzzled – then his expression hardened into one of contempt.

"Tennis balls, sire," he said.

"Tell your master," said Henry to the ambassador, "that we will come to France and play such a game with him that he will never forget. And when I am crowned king there, my glory will be so dazzling that he will be blinded by it." Henry looked around the council table. "So, then," he said, "it is to be war."

We will in France, by God's grace, play a set Shall strike his father's crown into the hazard

– Henry V

Preparing for War

Act two

Now all the youth of England are on fire
– *Chorus*

Word of Henry's decision swept through England like wildfire. Within days, all the men of fighting age were sharpening their swords and dreaming of the glory they would win in battle. They flocked to Southampton, where a fleet of ships waited to carry them across the sea to France.

Henry stood on the dockside, watching his army gather.

"What are our chances?" he asked the men standing next to him: the Earl of Cambridge, Lord Scroop and Sir Thomas Grey.

"We cannot fail, sire," said Scroop. "Everyone is loyal to you."

"Everyone?" said Henry. "Yesterday, a man was arrested for saying I'm a fool! But perhaps you're right. He didn't mean it; he'd probably had too much to drink. We should set him free."

"No, sire," said Cambridge. "Any hint of disloyalty must be severely punished."

"Very severely," said Grey.

"If I'm very severe with a man who has a big mouth, what punishments will I have left for real traitors?" Henry said, smiling.

"No, I'll set the poor fellow free. And now, here are your orders." Henry handed each of the men a letter. They opened them and immediately turned white and fell to their knees. The letters were warrants for their arrest on charges of high treason.

Henry's smile vanished instantly. "I trusted you," he said with cold fury, "and then I found out that you took money from the King of France to assassinate me!"

The men knew there was no point denying it. "Forgive us, sire!" they wailed.

You must not dare, for shame, to talk of mercy
– Henry V

"You didn't just betray me," spat Henry, "you betrayed all these brave men here. You betrayed England! I asked your advice about punishing traitors and you said be very severe. Well here's your punishment: death. Take them away."

The wretched traitors were dragged off. "They were the last obstacle," said Henry to his loyal lords. "Nothing can stop us now."

Excitement about the war had even reached Henry's old friends from his wild youth. Back in London, Pistol, the tavern-owner, and Bardolph, his red-faced friend, were getting ready to join the army.

They were packing their bags when Pistol's wife, Mistress Quickly, came running up.

"Come, all of you!" she cried. "Sir John Falstaff is dying." For all his rascally behaviour, Falstaff had a good heart, and had loved Henry like a son. He had never recovered from the moment when Henry became king and turned his back on him forever.

The friends all gathered upstairs around his sickbed. They could see that Falstaff was very weak. It seemed a long time since they had been drinking and joking with young Prince Hal.

When the clock struck midnight, the men went downstairs to stretch their legs. Soon they were quarrelling over an old bet.

Mistress Quickly and her serving boy came downstairs to join them. One look at her face was enough to tell them that Falstaff had died.

"I wish I could be with the old scoundrel," said Bardolph sadly, "even if he is in hell."

"He's not in hell," said Mistress Quickly. "He called upon God with his last breath."

"He called for wine with his last breath!" said the serving boy.

"Still, he was a good old soul," said Pistol, and everyone agreed. "But he's gone now and there's a war to fight in France, so we must leave. Goodbye, my love," he said to Mistress Quickly. He kissed her fondly.

"Take care of yourself and remember this above all things: always get paid in cash." he added.

The serving boy stood watching as the two men left the tavern. The moment they were out of sight, he tore off his apron and gave it to Mistress Quickly.

"I'm sorry," he said, "but I have to go with them." And he followed the men to Southampton, and war.

News that Henry was readying an army frightened the French king. He immediately dispatched his most powerful lords to strengthen France's defences against English invasion.

"Of course we should defend the kingdom," drawled the Dauphin, the king's son, "but Henry doesn't scare me. He's just a vain boy showing off."

"Never underestimate the English," said the king. "Remember Henry's great-uncle, the Black Prince. He was only young, but he slaughtered our army at the Battle of Crécy."

Before the Dauphin could answer, word came that Exeter had arrived with a message from Henry.

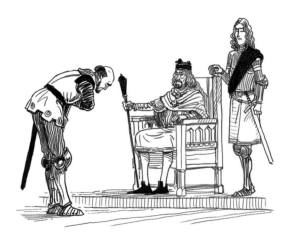

"Send him in," said the French king.

Exeter entered and bowed respectfully. "Your Majesty, my king instructs you to give up your crown, because he is the rightful King of France."

"And if I refuse?" said the king.

"Then my king will unleash the most terrible war," said Exeter grimly. "And your people will pay a dreadful price in blood and suffering. I also have a message for your Dauphin."

"What is it?" sneered the Dauphin. "My king's contempt," said Exeter. "He promises to make you pay on the battlefield for your insulting gift of tennis balls."

"I look forward to it," said the Dauphin coldly.

France

Act three

Henry's ships landed his army on the coast of France. Henry marched his men to the nearest town, the port of Harfleur, and laid siege to it. At his command, banks of artillery pounded its walls and, soon enough, tore a gaping hole in them.

Looking magnificent on his great white horse, Henry raised his sword, gave a loud cry and led a charge through the broken wall.

Once more unto the breach, dear friends,
Once more!
– Henry V

However his troops were beaten back by the town's defenders and many were killed.

Henry was about to launch a second attack when he saw that his men were now too scared to follow him. Henry realized that most of them had never been to war before. They had joined the army full of dreams of glory, and the frightening reality of combat had come as a dreadful shock. He had to inspire them or all would be lost.

"Again, brave Englishmen!" he cried. "Every one of you can be as fearsome as a tiger if you choose! Let's show the French how English heroes fight. For the honour of your fathers, who fought in these lands before you! For God, for England and your king!"

Follow your spirit, and upon this charge, Cry "God for Harry! England! And St George!"
         – Henry V

This gave his soldiers fresh heart.
They let out a terrifying roar and once
again charged towards the town.

Pistol, Bardolph and the serving boy
were among them. The king's words had
made them feel braver than before, but
nothing could banish their fear entirely.

Pistol sang a song to keep their
spirits up and the others joined
in as they neared their enemies.

Would I were
in an alehouse
in London!

– Boy

22

The fighting was hard and cruel and each felt sure he was going to die. Suddenly, in the din of battle, they heard a trumpet sound from the battlements of Harfleur. The Governor of the town wanted to talk. Henry ordered his troops to pull back.

"Do you surrender?" he asked. "Because this is your last chance." Henry knew that if he frightened the Governor into giving up, many lives would be saved.

The gates of
mercy shall be
all shut up
– Henry V

"If you resist us any longer, I swear that we will burn your town and slaughter everyone in it."

"We surrender," said the Governor. Henry breathed a sigh of relief. He had lost many men that day but still he had triumphed!

With Harfleur securely under his control, Henry set out to conquer the rest of France. Although he concealed it from his men, Henry was worried.

The siege had cost many soldiers' lives – and they had yet to meet the French army at full strength in battle.

Henry set his sights on Calais, a few days' march away. He would have to cross a river to get there, and the French might try to stop him by destroying the only bridge, so Henry sent some soldiers ahead to capture it and keep it safe.

A captain called Fluellen led them. The party took the bridge – and killed many Frenchmen – without losing a single English soldier. When the fighting was over, Pistol asked if he could speak with Fluellen.

"You're a good soldier, Pistol," said Fluellen.

"Thank you, sir," said Pistol, "but I have come to talk about my friend, Bardolph." Fluellen sighed. "The one condemned to death for stealing from a church on the way here?" he asked.

"Please, sir, Bardolph is a rascal but he doesn't deserve to die," said Pistol. "If you would only ask the Duke of Exeter to pardon him, he'll be no more trouble, I promise you."

"I'm sorry, Pistol," said Fluellen. "We cannot make exceptions where discipline is concerned or the army would fall to pieces."

Let gallows gape for dog, let man go free!

– Pistol

"But it's Bardolph!" begged Pistol. "You can't hang Bardolph!"

Fluellen was unmoved and Pistol realized it was hopeless.

Pistol cursed at Fluellen and then stormed off in a rage.

Before Fluellen could call Pistol back, King Henry arrived at the head of his army. It had taken the king longer than he had expected to reach the bridge. His soldiers were running low on food, and many had fallen ill; they were slowing down and getting weaker.

"Well done, Fluellen," said Henry, wearily. "How many men did we lose?"

"None, Your Majesty," said Fluellen. "Except for a red-faced fellow, name of Bardolph, who stole from a church and is to be hanged. Unless you want to pardon him, that is."

Henry remembered Bardolph, and all the
good times they had spent together in London,
but he knew he couldn't stop his execution.
If the French thought he'd allow his men
to loot their churches, they'd fight all the
harder against him. He shook his head.

"Then I will see it done," said Fluellen.

Trumpets sounded and a messenger
from the French king rode up.

"Your Majesty, my king bids
me tell you that he waits
nearby with a great army,"
said the messenger. "If
you do not return to
England at once, he
will make you pay
dearly for all the
French blood
you have spilt."

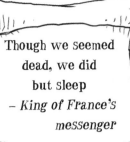

"Tell your master," said Henry, "that my army may be small and sick and hungry, but we are more than a match for any force he cares to send against us. I'm not looking for a fight, but if he comes near, we will destroy him."

Gloucester, Henry's brother, watched the messenger ride off.

"Was it wise, sire, to tell him how weak we are?" he asked. "If the French decide to attack, I do not believe we could beat them."

"We are in God's hands," said Henry. "Not theirs. The men have marched a long way and are tired. Tell them to pitch camp on the far side of the bridge."

If the English had any apprehension, they would run away
– Constable of France

That night in the French camp, the Dauphin and the French lords laughed and joked as they got ready to face Henry's troops the next day.

They knew they couldn't lose: the French army was larger and their soldiers were fitter, better fed and well rested. The battle they were about to fight was bound to go down in history as one of France's greatest victories.

The Battle of Agincourt

Act four

The English soldiers were camped so close to the French that they could hear their confident laughter on the night air. Men huddled gloomily around their fires, shaking with cold and fear. They were all dreading the dawn and the terrible defeat they were certain it would bring.

Henry knew he needed to raise their spirits, so he went around the camp, talking to as many of his soldiers as he could. He smiled and joked, and seemed so confident of victory that the men began to believe they might stand a chance.

But Henry was still
worried that some of
them were only pretending
to be brave in front of
their king. He wanted to
know how they truly felt,

so he pulled his hood down over his face
and, changing his voice, pretended to be an
ordinary soldier.

He went over to where three men
– John, Michael and Alexander – were
watching the sun rise.

"I don't think we will live long enough to see it go down again," said Michael sadly.

"If we're going to die," said Henry, "surely it's better to die for our king, and his just cause."

"We're poor men," said John. "How do we know whether his cause is just or not? We have to do what we're told."

"I tell you one thing, though," said Michael. "If it isn't just, the ghosts of all the men who are going to die for the king today will haunt him for the rest of his life!"

"I heard the king say he'd rather die than be taken prisoner," said Henry.

If the cause be not good, the king himself hath a heavy reckoning to make
– Michael

"He can say what he likes," said Michael, "but once we're dead he can change his mind and it'll be too late for us!"

Henry knew he had to keep pretending,
but Michael was making him very angry.
"If we weren't about to fight a battle,"
Henry said, "I'd punish you for your
disloyalty."

"If we are still alive by evening," said
Michael, "feel free to try. Here's my glove;
give me one of yours and wear it in your
helmet – that way we'll be able to find
each other again."

"Never mind that now!" said John. "It's
the French we should be fighting, not one
another – so let's be friends. The time has
come for battle."

The men went off to get ready, leaving Henry alone. "Oh, how I envy them!" he thought. "A poor man only has himself to worry about. A king must worry about everybody he rules over, and that worry never ends."

Henry returned to his tent, ready to fight. "God of war," he prayed. "Please give my soldiers courage today."

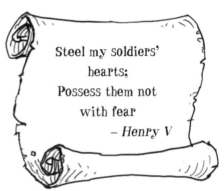

Steel my soldiers' hearts;
Possess them not with fear
– Henry V

There was great excitement among the French as the noblemen took to their horses.

"One look at you, my lords," said their commander, "and the poor ragged English will be so scared a single breath would blow them over! We won't even need the infantry!"

In Henry's camp, Exeter and the rest of his generals shook hands and wished each other well, but they knew that they had little hope of victory.

"They have sixty thousand men," said Westmorland.

"They outnumber us five to one," said Exeter.

"If only we had more men!" Westmorland sighed.

"I don't want one more man in my army," said Henry. "Truly. If we lose this battle, the fewer of us that die, the better. If we win, imagine the glory we'll have earned! Today is St Crispin's day, isn't it? Mark my words: every St Crispin's day from now until the end of time will be a celebration of the great victory we are about to win.

We few – we happy few – we band of brothers! Because anyone who fights with me today will be my brother, I don't care how poor he is. And the great men of England who are not here among us now will think themselves cursed that they missed this chance to win eternal glory!"

And Crispin Crispian shall ne'er go by From this day to the ending of the world But we in it shall be remembered!
– Henry V

With these inspiring words, Henry sent his men charging into battle. The French were expecting a hungry rabble. When they saw a ferocious horde racing towards them they were taken entirely by surprise.

Pistol looked so fierce on the battlefield that the first French soldier he met thought he had run into the bravest knight in England – and he fell to his knees and surrendered on the spot!

English archers made short work of the proud French horsemen. Without their officers to command them, the rest of the French army didn't know what to do.

The Dauphin was in despair. "Shame on us all!" he cried, as he looked around his bloody and bewildered countrymen. "We should never have underestimated King Henry!"

All is confounded, all!
Mortal reproach and everlasting shame
Sits mocking in our plumes
– Dauphin

Still the fighting went on and many brave men on both sides lost their lives.

After hours of killing, Henry was exhausted and sick of the slaughter. When he saw another Frenchman riding towards him on a horse, he couldn't believe his eyes.

"Haven't you had enough yet?" he screamed. "Will you only be happy when we have killed every one of you?"

"Forgive me, great king," said the man, humbly. Henry realized that this was the messenger who had threatened him so confidently just the day before. "My master, the King of France surrenders; you have won. All he asks now is that we may gather and bury our dead."

For a moment, Henry didn't know what to say. Then he sank to his knees and cried, "Thank God!"

The day is yours
– King of France's
messenger

When the dead were counted, Henry was told that ten thousand Frenchmen had been killed. The English had lost only a few hundred.

Michael kept his promise and came looking for the man who had taken his glove. When he realized that he'd been arguing with the king himself, he was frightened and begged to be forgiven.

But Henry smiled and ordered that the glove he had given to Michael should be filled with gold. Michael was a brave Englishman and on this glorious day deserved no less.

Peace

Act five

Henry returned to London in triumph. The narrow streets filled with people cheering his name and straining to get a glimpse of him.

The homecoming was not so happy for others. Pistol learned that Mistress Quickly had fallen ill and died while they were away.

Losing her so soon after the death of his friend Bardolph hardened Pistol's heart. He forgot all dreams of soldierly glory and returned to his wicked old life as a thief.

The war was over, but Henry had yet to agree the terms for peace. He and his lords went back to France in great splendour to meet the French king.

The meeting took place in the Duke of Burgundy's castle.

"Your Majesty," said the Duke to Henry, "until we sign a peace treaty, we cannot release our men from the army. That means there is no one to till the fields, no one to harvest the crops."

"We have made our demands," said Henry, "if you want peace, you must agree to them."

"Surely, sire, you will be generous in victory," said Burgundy, "and there are some things you have asked for that we cannot agree to."

"Very well," said Henry. "Here are my most trusted lords. Talk to them about it and whatever they agree to, I will agree to. There is only one thing I will not give up."

"What is that?" asked Burgundy.

Henry looked across the room at the King of France's beautiful daughter.

"Princess Katherine over there," he said. "I want to marry her."

Burgundy smiled, and so did the King of France, who said, "Then perhaps we should leave you two alone together."

If you will love me soundly with your French heart, I will be glad to hear you confess it brokenly with your English tongue
– Henry V

Katherine had heard about the dashing young English king. She was so interested in him that she'd asked her maid, who had lived in England, to teach her the language. But alone with him for the first time, she felt very shy.

Henry was little better.

"I'm just a rough soldier," he said eventually. "I wish I had the words to tell you how I feel about you."

"I cannot love an enemy of France," said Katherine.

"I am not an enemy of France," said Henry, "I love France. If I marry you, our two great countries will become friends after so many years of fighting. So then, will you be my queen?"

Katherine blushed and nodded her head. Henry leaned in to kiss her but she pulled back. "It is not the fashion in France for high-born ladies to kiss," she said.

"What do we care about that?" said Henry. "We are the ones who set the fashions!" and he took her in his arms and kissed her.

And so it was that Henry V married Katherine and forged a great alliance with France.

But it was not to last. Henry was a strong king but he died young, leaving his son to become king when he was only a baby. King Henry VI was too young, and too weak, to maintain peace. During his reign, bloody civil war tore England apart.

Everything that Henry V had fought for – at the cost of so many lives and so much suffering – was lost.

Small time, but in that small most greatly lived This star of England
— Chorus

The end

To my 3 children xxx Love Daddy
Hamet
Jedah
Susanih
and
more!

Consultant: Dr Tamsin Badcoe
Editors: Ruth Symons and Carly Madden
Designer: Andrew Crowson
Project Designer: Rachel Lawston
Editorial Director: Victoria Garrard
Art Director: Laura Roberts-Jensen

Copyright © QED Publishing 2015

First published in the UK in 2015 by
QED Publishing
A Quarto Group company
The Old Brewery
6 Blundell Street
London N7 9BH

www.qed-publishing.co.uk

A catalogue record for this book is available from the British Library.

ISBN 978 1 78493 005 9

Printed in China